Helicopter

For: Vicki, Lily, Edward, and Tilly.

Rockpool Children's Books
15 North Street
Marton
Warwickshire
CV23 9RJ

First published in Great Britain by Rockpool Children's Books Ltd. 2008
Text and Illustrations copyright © Stuart Trotter / Design Concept Elaine Lonergan 2007
Stuart Trotter has asserted the moral rights
to be identified as the author and illustrator of this book.

A CIP catalogue record of this book is available
from the British Library.

Printed in China

rockpool
children's books

A Lift the Flap Book

Stuart Trotter & Elaine Lonergan

Helicopter

This is Helicopter.

Through the wind
and rain and snow,
He flies to places others don't go!

Above the rooves
our hero flies

Some walkers lost in deep white snow.

Lift
the
Flap

As Helicopter
hovers with a
"THUMP, THUMP"sound,

In stormy seas
a boat goes down,

Lift
the
Flap

One last wave,
no time to stay,

Lift the Flap

"Phew!" thought Helicopter.
"What an exciting day."
He'd heard Police Car
had been busy too....
but that's another story!

Brave and strong, kind and true,
Rescue Team is there for you!